LADYBIRD BOOKS

UK | USA | Canada | Ireland | Australia
India | New Zealand | South Africa
Ladybird Books is part of the Penguin Random House group of companies
whose addresses can be found at global.penguinrandomhouse.com.

www.penguin.co.uk   www.puffin.co.uk   www.ladybird.co.uk

Penguin
Random House
UK

First published 1999
Reissued 2012 as part of the Ladybird First Favourite Tales series
This Ladybird Picture Books edition published 2015
005

Copyright © Ladybird Books Ltd, 1999

Printed in China

The authorized representative in the EEA is Penguin Random House Ireland
Morrison Chambers, 32 Nassau Street, Dublin D02 YH68

A CIP catalogue record for this book is available from the British Library

ISBN: 978–0–723–28661–5

All correspondence to:
Ladybird Books, Penguin Random House Children's
One Embassy Gardens, 8 Viaduct Gardens, London SW11 7BW

Ladybird Picture Books

The Three Billy Goats Gruff

BASED ON A TRADITIONAL FOLK TALE

retold by Irene Yates ★ illustrated by Ailie Busby

Once upon a time there were three
billy goats Gruff, Gruff, Gruff,
who said, "This grass isn't good enough!
We need to look for pastures new,
where the grass is sweet and delicious to chew."

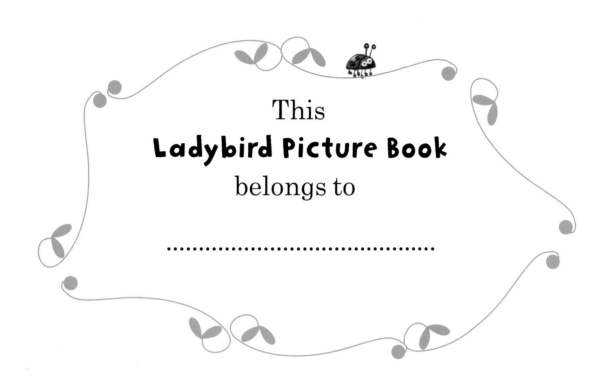

This
Ladybird Picture Book
belongs to

....

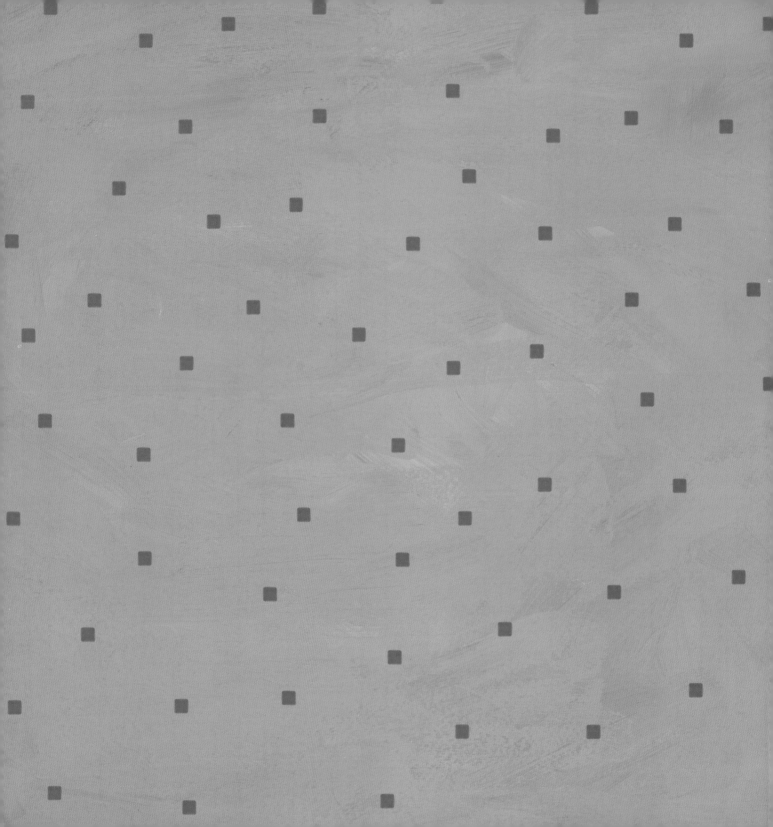

Off they trotted till they came to a river,
where they saw . . .

...across the water, a meadow green,
with the sweetest grass they had ever seen.

The goats longed to cross the bridge, but...

a wicked old troll lived underneath,
with horrible claws and terrible teeth,
and he gobbled up anyone trying to cross.

Soon the littlest billy goat Gruff said,
"I'm off across the bridge to eat that sweet grass!"

And off he trotted with a trip trap, trip trap,
across the wooden planks.

The wicked old troll sharpened his claws and gnashed his teeth, and ...

...UP he popped with a monstrous growl!

"WHO'S THAT TRIP-TRAPPING OVER MY BRIDGE?"

"It's only me," said the littlest billy goat Gruff. "Please let me pass, to eat the green grass!"

But the troll growled, "No! No! I'M going to eat YOU instead!"

"Oh, please don't!" said the littlest billy goat. "Just wait a while! The second billy goat will make you smile! He's much, much bigger and fatter than I!"

And the troll thought, "Mmmmm ... that's worth a try!"

So the littlest billy goat Gruff skipped over the bridge and into the meadow.

Soon the middle-sized billy goat Gruff
said, "I'm off across the bridge to eat that
sweet grass!"

And off he trotted with a trip trap, trip trap,
across the wooden planks.

The wicked old troll sharpened his claws and gnashed his teeth, and ...

...UP he popped with a deafening roar!

"WHO'S THAT TRIP-TRAPPING OVER
MY BRIDGE?"

"It's only me," said the middle-sized billy goat Gruff.
"Please let me pass, to eat the green grass!"

But the troll roared, "No! No! I'M going to eat
YOU instead!"

"Oh, please don't!" said the middle-sized billy goat. "Just wait a while! The third billy goat will make you smile! He's much, much bigger and fatter than I!"

And the troll thought, "Mmmmm . . . that's worth a try!"

So the middle-sized billy goat Gruff skipped over the bridge and into the meadow.

Soon the **big** billy goat Gruff said, "I'm off across the bridge to eat that sweet grass!"

And off he trotted with a trip trap, trip trap, across the wooden planks.

The wicked old troll sharpened his claws and gnashed his teeth, and . . .

...UP he popped with a fearful holler!

"WHO'S THAT TRIP-TRAPPING OVER MY BRIDGE?"

"It's ME!" said the big billy goat Gruff. "I'm going past to eat the green grass!"

But the troll hollered, "No! No! I'M going to eat YOU instead!"

And the third billy goat said, in a voice like thunder ...

"OH NO, YOU'RE NOT!"

Down went the billy goat's head ...

nd up went the wicked
troll into the air and
over the bridge he fell …

...SPLASH!

into the river,
never to be seen again!

Then the **big** billy goat Gruff skipped across the bridge to join his brothers.

And the three billy goats munched happily in pastures new, saying, "Mmmmm . . . this grass is so good to chew!"

MUNCH!

MUNCH!

MUNCH!

Ladybird Picture Books

Look out for...

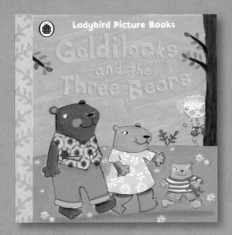

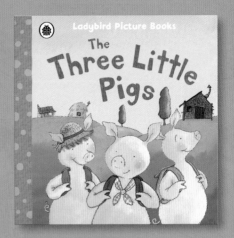